Professor von Schmell

and his

Fart Powered Bike

Words by Leon Howlett Pictures by James Gibson

First published in the UK in 2020 by Stour Valley Publishing
This edition published in 2022 by the Author/Illustrator via KDP

Text Copyright © Leon Howlett 2020
Illustrations Copyright © James Gibson 2020

A CIP Catalogue Record of this book is available from the British Library

For Lily and Louis, Noah and Iris, Hollie and Harrison.
'The little farts'

For Coryn and Mason, Brooke and Owen, Dylan and
Astrid, Morgan and Darcy
'The big farts'

For Michelle -You are my BEST. DAY. EVER!!
Every single day.

Professor von Schmell is
a little bit odd

He lives in a tower that
looks like a cod

At the top of his tower,
is a dark, damp room

and that's where he sits
all day in the gloom

inventing weird things
to sell to the people

all alone, in the dark.
in his big fishy steeple

The things that he makes
are silly, for sure

A bowl that cleans cups
and a self-opening door

and his latest invention
is one you will like...

A magnificent...

two-wheeled...

FART-POWERED...

BIKE!

The fart-powered bike runs on
beans and brown rice

just fill up the tank
and then stir it round twice

Start up the engine
and sit on the seat

and with a huge
FAAAAAARRRRRTTTT
you whizz off down the street

Now... one gloomy morning
on a miserable day

a poster went up
which had something to say

"One lap of the town.

A race!

Do you dare?"

"The winner is promised
a glorious prize!

One week on the beautiful
Isle of Blue Skies"

The Professor he gasped
and his eyes they lit up

He laughed as he drank
from his grimy brown cup

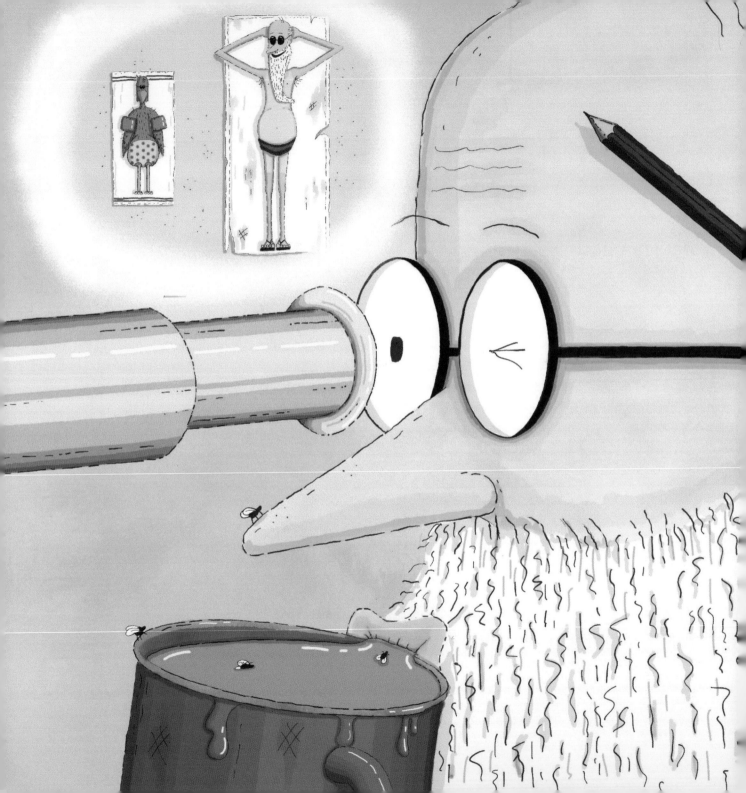

"This is my chance
if I take part in this race

to beat my old foe,
Professor von Ace!"

Now, Professor von Ace thought
he was better by far
Driving around in his silly 'Burp Car'

"My Fart Bike can win,
it can beat his Burp Car
and then I'll be off on my hols
Mwahahahaaaa!"

On the day of the race
each Professor lined up

Professors from all over
the town of Mud-lup

Each with their own crazy invention
Eager to win.
Of that, there's no question.

As Professor von Schmell
was stirring his tank

he spotted von Ace and his heart
well... it SANK!

For von Ace was holding
some 'Triple-Eggs' Cola

(the strongest burp-drink
from the Hills of Trimbola)

With his burp power he will win
that much is for certain

My dreams of a holiday
have gone for a burton

Hold on, hold up.
Don't worry, have no fear.

Professor von Schmell
had a splendid idea.

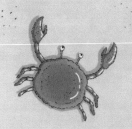

He remembered Granny Schmell's
famous STINK sprouts

With this plan, if it works, he will
win.
There's no doubt!

"Back home, in the cupboard.
I'll dash back and get them"

Oh no! It's the Mayor.
He's called their attention!

"The race will begin
on the count of three"

"Oh no" cried von Schmell,
"There's no time! Woe is me."

"With Ace's burp-power
he will win. I'm no match!"

Yet as the Mayor counted
a new plan did Schmell hatch

"THREE" the Mayor yelled
and the race it was started

"GO!" screamed the crowd
as the fart bike farted

BUUUUURRRRPPPP went von Ace
who shot into the lead

"Granny's Sprouts"
thought von Schmell
"That's what I need!"

And the plan that was formed
was then put in place

on the penultimate corner
near the end of the race

As the race pack went past
von Schmell's codfish tower

he let out a "SQUAWK"
with all of his power.

"SQUAWK SQUAWK!
SQUAWK SQUAWK!"

he continued to yell

at home, von Schmell's parrot
(whose name we can't tell)

heard von Schmell's squawks
and fell from his bell!

Parrot news
(REPEAT)

Up to the larder
clever parrot flew

for he heard every squawk
and von Schmell's plan he knew

Grabbing the sprouts
in an old rusty case

he flew out of the window
and joined in the race

Over the fart-bike
and into a hover

he dropped all the sprouts
without any bother

von Schmell opened his tank
and in they all fell

FAAAAAAAARRRRRTTTT
went the bike and...

EWWWW...
What a SMELL!

The fart-bike leapt forward
at a frightening pace

Zipped past the Burp Car
and into...

FIRST PLACE!

"Woohoo" von Schmell cried
"Those sprouts were enough"

"We've won the first prize with

a...

big...

stinky...

The End.

Leon Howlett

Leon lives two lives.
In one he drives trains and eats pickled onion monster munch.
In the other, he imagines crazy stories and writes them down...
and still eats pickled onion monster munch.
Leon lives out both of these lives in a sleepy little village in Essex with
his wife and two children...near to a shop that sells pickled onion
monster munch.

James Gibson

James Gibson is a genius, his fingertips are gold
He can make fantastic pictures when a story he is told
He uses paints and toothpicks, his fingers or a knife
To take your wildest dreams and then bring them all to life.

Join the Professor and Parrot again
soon
in their next adventure:

Professor von Schmell
and the
Garden PooCano

Printed in Great Britain
by Amazon